# ✳ GOOD ✳ NIGHT ✳
# DINOSAURS

### BY JUDY SIERRA
### ILLUSTRATED BY VICTORIA CHESS

#### CLARION BOOKS ✳ NEW YORK

For Kosta Horaites
—J. S.

*  *  *  *  *

For Phoebe, with love
—V. C.

The sun sank low
        in the Mesozoic sky.
It was bedtime—
        bedtime for dinosaurs.

Tiny stegosauruses
Whispered creepy stories
Of the monsters in the forests
To trembling allosauruses.

Soon those scaredysauruses

Were snoring all in choruses

While snoozing

    In the sweet

        soft

           ooze.


Good night, dinosaurs.

Sleep tight, dinosaurs.

Good night,

    dinosaurs,

        good night.

Two naughty young diplodocus
Screamed and made a dreadful fuss—

"We do not wish to brush our teeth!
To wash our necks would take a week!
We'd rather just play hide and seek."

Mom and Dad diplodocus
(Each one was bigger than a bus)
Chased them off to bed with hisses,
Followed by diplodokisses.

Good night, dinosaurs,
Don't fight, dinosaurs,
Good night,
     dinosaurs,
         good night.

Pteranodons
Put their nightgowns on.
There were bottles all around,

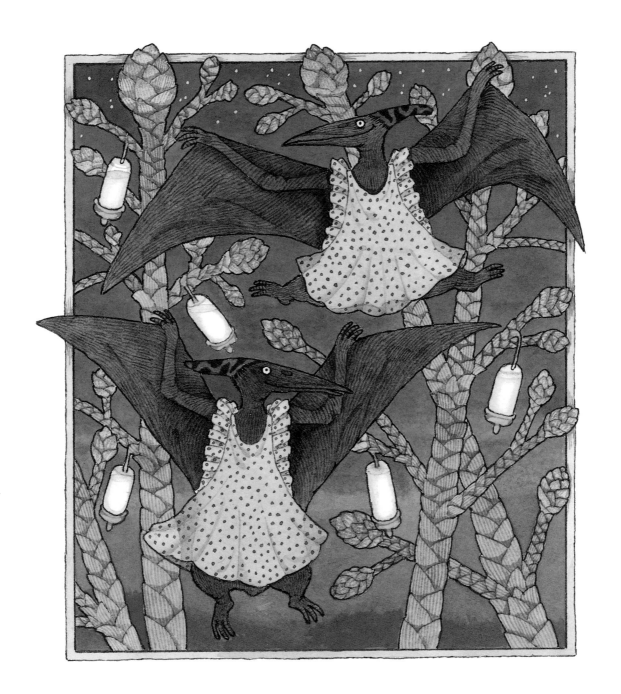

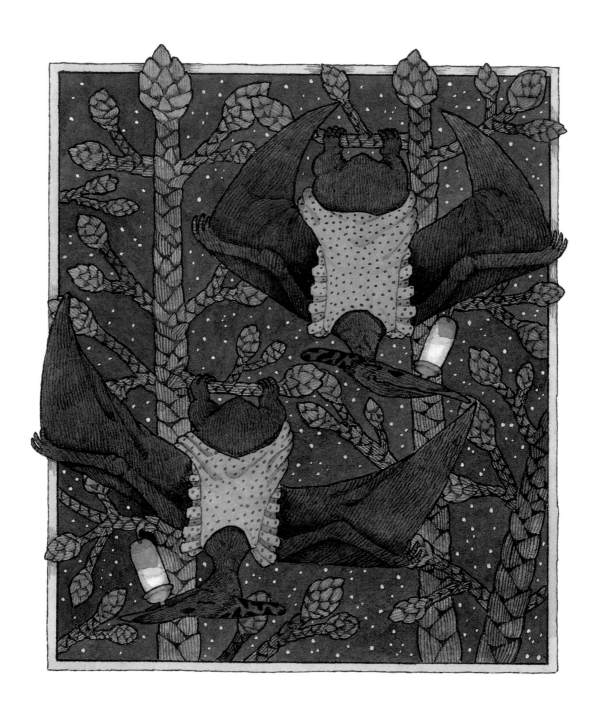

They were swinging upside down,
Forty feet above the ground,
Softly swaying to the sound
Of the dinosaurs' sleepytime song.

Good night, dinosaurs,
Hold on tight, dinosaurs,
Good night,
        dinosaurs,
                good night.

Three tyrannosaurus rexes
Once lay dreaming of their breakfasts
In what's now the state of Texas.

Then each fearsome future fossil
Yawned a yawn that was colossal;
As the moon lit up the sky,
And they nestled side by side,
Tyrannograndma sang that lizard lullaby.

Good night, dinosaurs,
Don't bite, dinosaurs,
Good night,
        dinosaurs,
                good night.

Just-hatched baby compsognathus,
With crinkly wrinkly baby faces,
Twitched their tails
And sucked their claws.
Amidst their family's "ooh's" and "aah's"
They opened up their tiny jaws,
Said their very first word,

*peep*

Closed their eyes,
      and fell asleep.

Rockabye, dinosaurs,
Don't cry, dinosaurs,
Good night,
      dinosaurs,
         good night.

Ten very tired triceratops
Sucked on seaweed lollipops
While sitting in a squishy fishy tub.
Their papa rubbed their scales,
And scrubbed their ticklish tails,
Until everybody yelled

PLEASE STOP!

Then they cuddled up together
By that prehistoric river
Till their eye-
                    lids
                         dropped.

Good night, dinosaurs,
Shiny bright dinosaurs,
Good night,
        dinosaurs,
                good night.

And then Jupiter and Mars,
And a thousand shooting stars,
Sparkled in the night,
Sprinkling down their light
On that heap
        of sleeping reptiles
                in their

        Home Sweet Swamp.

Good night, dinosaurs,
Sleep tight, dinosaurs,
Good night,
        dinosaurs,
                good night.

CLARION BOOKS
A Houghton Mifflin Company imprint
215 Park Avenue South, New York, NY 10003
Text copyright © 1996 by Judy Sierra
Illustrations copyright © 1996 by Victoria Chess

Illustrations executed in watercolors
Type is 13 point Bookman

For information about this and other Houghton Mifflin trade and
reference books and multimedia products, visit The Bookstore at
Houghton Mifflin on the World Wide Web at
(http://www.hmco.com/trade/).

Printed in Hong Kong
Book design by Sylvia Frezzolini Severance

LIBRARY OF CONGRESS CATALOGING-IN-PUBLICATION DATA
Sierra, Judy.  Good night, dinosaurs / by Judy Sierra;
illustrated by Victoria Chess.
p.  cm.
Summary: Verses describe the bedtime preparations
of different kinds of dinosaurs.
ISBN 0-395-65016-X
1. Dinosaurs—Juvenile poetry. 2. Night—Juvenile poetry. 3.
Children's poetry, American.  [1. Dinosaurs—Poetry.
2. Bedtime—Poetry. 3. American poetry.]
I. Chess, Victoria, ill. II. Title.
PS3569.I39G66   1995                   93-8855
811'.54—dc20                              CIP
                                                 AC
DNH  10 9 8 7 6 5 4 3 2 1

811
SIE      Sierra, Judy

         Good night, di-
         nosaurs

| DUE DATE | BRODART | 08/96 | 14.45 |
|---|---|---|---|
| OCT 3 3 | | | |
| OCT 2 | | | |
| OCT 2 8 | | | |
| NOV 7 | | | |
| NOV 2 2 | | | |
| ~~Woodbck~~ | | | |
| MAY 8 4 | | | |
| | | | |
| | | | |
| | | | |
| | | | |